GRANNY GERT
AND THE BUNION BROTHERS

BY DOTTI ENDERLE
ILLUSTRATED BY JOE KULKA

PELICAN PUBLISHING COMPANY

GRETNA 2006

The word "Pelican" and the depiction of a pelican are trademarks
of Pelican Publishing Company, Inc., and are registered in the
U.S. Patent and Trademark Office.

Library of Congress Cataloging-in-Publication Data

Enderle, Dotti, 1954-
  Granny Gert and the Bunion Brothers / by Dotti Enderle ; illustrated by Joe
Kulka.
       p. cm.
  Summary: When "the dumbest boys in Texas" both fall in love with the
granddaughter of their new employer, they shirk their duties to fight over the
beautiful Starla until Granny Gert threatens to sic Mad Dog on them.
  ISBN-13: 978-1-58980-373-2 (hardcover : alk. paper)
  [1. Brothers—Fiction. 2. Love—Fiction. 3. Texas—Fiction. 4. Tall tales.] I.
Kulka, Joe, ill. II. Title.
  PZ7.E69645Gra 2006
  [E]—dc22

                                        2006009787

Printed in China
Published by Pelican Publishing Company, Inc.
1000 Burmaster Street, Gretna, Louisiana 70053

GRANNY GERT AND THE
BUNION BROTHERS

Texas is a mighty big place, so to say the
Bunion Brothers were the dumbest boys in Texas
would be saying a lot. But the truth is—they
were! Buddy and Buck Bunion not only lacked in
the brains department, but they were worthless
rascals as well. They had only one talent between
them—playing the banjo.

Once, after being chased out of Amarillo,

the Bunion Brothers headed southeast,

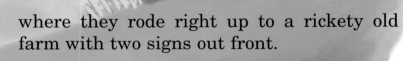

where they rode right up to a rickety old farm with two signs out front.

Figuring it best to approach with caution, they rapped lightly on the door. It swung open in a hurry.

"State your business, varmints."

The boys took a step back. "We're the Bunion Brothers, ma'am," Buck said. "And we're looking for work."

Granny eyed them, rubbing the whisker on her chin. "Well, I could use some stout boys like you to clean my privy."

Buddy and Buck jumped at the offer like a couple of hound dogs on a ham. "Yes, ma'am!"

"Come on in first and have some dewberry cobbler," Granny offered. "You'll need your strength. And be sure to wipe your feet, or I'll sic Mad Dog on you."

The Bunion Brothers didn't want to take any chances. They slipped off their boots and stepped inside Granny's farmhouse.

On their way to the kitchen, they bumped into the loveliest vision of a girl ever to step foot on Texas soil. Both boys stood staring, too stunned to apologize.

"It's a princess, come out of a fairy tale," Buddy said with a sigh.

"It's an angel, come down from Heaven," Buck said in a whisper.

"It's my granddaughter, Starla Scissors, come to live with me," Granny Gert said with a growl. "And you better behave yourselves, or I'll sic Mad Dog on you."

But Granny's words were wasted on the Bunion Brothers. It was love, pure and simple. They both had eyes for Starla.

After shoveling down two helpings of cobbler each, the boys followed Granny out to their new work quarters, also known as the outhouse.

"Make it shine, boys," Granny said.

They set to it, scrubbing and cleaning. They didn't stop once, not even to read the catalog hanging by the door.

After supper, Buck and Buddy found their chance to impress Starla. They pulled out their banjo and commenced to pickin' and singin'.

Starla, my darling,
You've gone to my head.
You're as tasty as gravy
And as fine as cornbread.
Your lips are like cherries;
Your eyes are like moons.
You're as cute and as cuddly
As a ring-tailed raccoon.

"Goodness, boys!" Granny said. "Your singing is so sour, it pickled the cucumbers!"

But Starla batted her eyes, and the Bunion Brothers' hearts melted like butter on a flapjack.

The next day, Granny set the boys to white-washing the fence. Before long Buck said, "I think I'll slip around and get a dipper of water." He slipped around all right, around and into the parlor where Starla sat.

Buck knelt down in front of her. "Miss Starla, when I'm near you, I hear bells ringing in my heart."

"You're gonna be hearing more than bells when I sic Mad Dog on you," threatened Granny. "Now get back to work!"

Buck backed away, blowing kisses to Starla as he left.

A little while later, Buddy said, "I'm just going to run in and get another paintbrush." He ran— straight into the parlor.

"Oh, Starla," he said. "You've got me so crazy in love, I don't know which end is up."

"Guess which end is stinging!" Granny said. "Now scoot out of here before I sic Mad Dog on you!"

Buddy hurried out the back door, but he was met by Buck, fighting mad, with ears as red as chili peppers. "I thought you were going in for a paintbrush."

Buddy looked his brother in the eyes. "I gotta fess up. I'm in love with Starla, and I intend to marry her."

"What are you talking about?" asked Buck. "Starla's mine. She belongs to me!"

Buddy's nostrils flared like a bull. "No. She loves me! Don't you see the way she looks at me?"

"Yep," Buck said. "Like a mouse that's just seen a cat! Besides, she loves me."

"Well, you can't have her!"

"Neither can you!"

For the first time in their miserable lives, the Bunion Brothers raised their fists against each other.

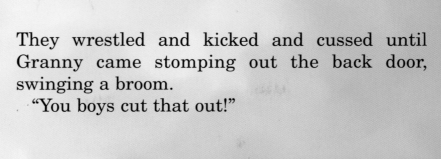

They wrestled and kicked and cussed until
Granny came stomping out the back door,
swinging a broom.

"You boys cut that out!"

Buddy and Buck knew not to mess with Granny. They stood up, straight as clothesline poles.

"Sit down," Granny said. "We need to have a heart to heart."

Since the Bunion Brothers preferred talking to Granny more than getting walloped by her, they quickly sat down on the steps.

Granny leaned in so close, they could smell the grits on her breath. "You should be ashamed of yourselves," she said. "Blood is thicker than water. You're brothers, for goodness sake. That should mean something. Don't ever let anything come between the two of you."

Buck looked at Buddy. Buddy looked at Buck. Then they each started to blubber like a baby in a day-old diaper.

"I'm sorry."

"No, it's my fault."

"That's better," Granny said. "Now stop your sniveling and come have a glass of lemonade."

They followed Granny into the kitchen, but there sat Starla, pretty as a gold nugget in a muddy stream. Suddenly, the brothers forgot how thick their blood was.

"She's mine!"
"No, mine!"
Granny Gert threw her hands in the air.
"That's it! I'm siccing Mad Dog on you!"

The Bunion Brothers decided their love for Starla wasn't nearly as strong as their fear of Mad Dog. They trampled each other getting to the front door, where they bumped into the loveliest vision of a girl ever to set foot on Texas soil, the mirror image of Starla.

"Scarlett!" Starla called from behind them. "You're here at last!" The Scissors Sisters gave each other a squeezy hug.

MAD DOG

With Scarlett's arrival, the Bullion Brothers decided to stay, retaining their jobs as Granny's Chief Outhouse Keepers and Fence Painters. Every night they would court Starla and Scarlett with their banjo.

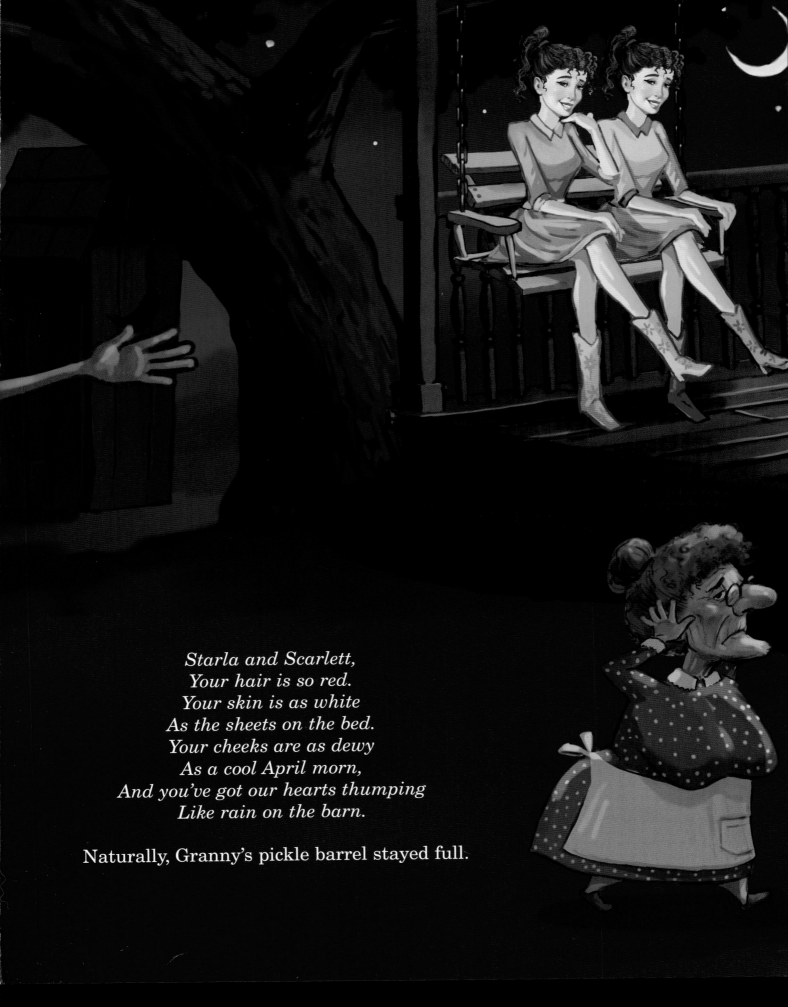

Starla and Scarlett,
Your hair is so red.
Your skin is as white
As the sheets on the bed.
Your cheeks are as dewy
As a cool April morn,
And you've got our hearts thumping
Like rain on the barn.

Naturally, Granny's pickle barrel stayed full.

But late at night, when everyone was snug asleep, Granny would take Mad Dog for a walk. And if she was in a good mood, she'd even let him wallow in the mire.